This Book presented to

TEMPLE
ISRAEL

in honor of

BRENDA CURLAND

from

Joshua Buchman

Hanukkah 1992

Moose Street

By Anne Mazer

ALFRED A. KNOPF ⋙ NEW YORK

THIS IS A BORZOI BOOK PUBLISHED BY ALFRED A. KNOPF, INC.

Library of Congress Cataloging-in-Publication Data

Mazer, Anne.
    Moose Street / by Anne Mazer.
        p.   cm.
    Summary: Eleven-year-old Lena, the only Jewish child on Moose
Street, sees life as an insider and an outsider.
        ISBN 0-679-83233-5 (trade) — ISBN 0-679-93233-X (lib. bdg.)
        [1. Jews—Fiction. 2. City and town life—Fiction.] I. Title.
PZ7.M47396Mo   1992
[Fic]—dc20   91-36534

Manufactured in the United States of America
10   9   8   7   6   5   4   3   2   1

For Andy — A. M.

Moose Street

Contents

Jefferson Square Park

It was Lena's morning to baby-sit. She put Deedee in the old big-wheeled black carriage with the creaky hood that stuck when you opened or shut it.

Lena covered the baby with a faded yellow blanket. Her sister's light brown hair curled around her neck and ears. Her eyes were shut, her rosy mouth slightly open, and her plump hand clutched a green toothbrush. She was already asleep.

"Be back for lunch!" Lena's mother called. "Stay in the park, and don't leave Deedee alone for a minute!"

"Don't worry, Mom." Lena tucked a bottle into one corner of the carriage. Three dimes jingled in her pocket.

"And no candy!"

"No candy," Lena echoed.

The big creaky carriage was hard to push. Lena made her way slowly down Moose Street humming a tune.

The August day was hot but not sticky. Lena turned the corner past Nancy's house and stopped in front of Catalano's candy store. She parked the carriage on the grass and ran up the stairs.

"One grape Popsicle, please."

"Five cents," said Mr. Catalano, who reminded Lena of a marshmallow bunny, all round and soft, with little red-rimmed eyes.

Lena put a dime on the wooden counter. She loved the sweet-tasting liquid in tiny wax bottles, the sticks of red and black licorice, the banana-flavored necklaces that you could

4

both wear and eat. Every time that Lena had some money she spent it here.

Mr. Catalano dropped the dime into the cash register and slid a nickel across the counter to Lena.

"And a bag of M&M's," said Lena. She slid the nickel back across the counter and put the candy into her pocket.

On the stairs she peeled the translucent white paper with orange letters off the Popsicle and took the first careful lick.

She skipped down to the carriage.

"Mama?"

"Sshhhh . . . Go back to sleep." Lena hooked her elbows around the carriage handle so she could walk and eat her Popsicle at the same time and headed for the park. She hoped Nancy would be there. Sometimes her friend had to spend the day with her grandmother.

"Hello, dear." It was a nun from St. Mary's

with a big wooden cross hanging from her neck.

"Hello," Lena mumbled. Should she have said, "Hello, Sister," as Nancy did? It seemed rude not to say more. But the nun was not her sister.

Nancy made the sign of the cross whenever she met a priest or a nun on the street, and she showed Lena how to do it too. But Lena could never bring herself to make the sign of the cross, even to see what it would feel like.

Did the nun know she was Jewish? Would she still have said hello if she knew? Would she have tried to convert her? Did it bother her that Lena didn't make the sign of the cross?

And was she really bald under that black and white headpiece?

"Lena!" The twins, Mary Catherine and Catherine Mary, dressed in spotless matching outfits of yellow and pink, skipped out of the park.

"We just won the hopscotch tournament," announced Mary Catherine, the pink twin.

"This is what we got," said Catherine Mary, the yellow twin, holding up a box of colored chalk.

The twins skipped up the street. Lena took another lick from the Popsicle and turned the carriage into Jefferson Square Park.

Three boys were throwing sand at one another, a couple of girls wobbled on stilts, and some kids were sitting at a table making cabins out of Popsicle sticks. A group of teenage boys sat by the stone fountain with its trough of stagnant green water that you could smell clear across the park.

It should really be called Jefferson Round Park, thought Lena as she wheeled the carriage toward the swings. The park was a circle bounded by a street—an island of kids in a sea of painted two-family wooden houses. It was the hub, the center of the neighborhood. Everyone met there. In the winter there were snow forts and ice-skating; in the summer, hopscotch, Hula-Hoop, and roller-skating contests and crafts with high school kids hired as counselors by the city.

In the summer Lena went almost every day.

The first person she saw was Esther Brown, clutching a small paper bag to her chest.

"Hi," said Lena.

"Hey," muttered Esther. She wouldn't meet Lena's eyes.

Why did Esther slouch when she could skip or run? Lena wondered. Why did she keep her eyes on the ground when the sky was clear and fresh, and boys and girls shouted from one end of the park to another?

"See you later?" Lena called after her. Though she couldn't remember ever seeing Esther in the park for more than five minutes.

Esther didn't answer.

Lena shrugged and pushed the carriage farther into the park.

At one of the picnic tables, Roseanne, who lived across the street from Lena, was painting her nails bright red.

Roseanne was sixteen. She was short and had long black hair. Two years ago she used to baby-sit when Lena's parents went out. She always brought her curlers and her hair dryer—a pink plastic bonnet with a white hose—and set her hair and Lena's with lots of shiny pink gel. Lena loved touching the tight round curls of hair just after the curlers had been taken out. The curls felt sticky and firm until Roseanne brushed them. Then Lena's hair fell in soft graceful waves over her neck and shoulders.

"Hi, Roseanne!" she called.

"Hey, Lena." Roseanne waved her wet nails in the air.

"Lena! Lena!" From under an elm tree Nancy waved a stick at her. "Over here!"

The heavy black carriage creaked and muttered as Lena pushed it over the grass. She parked it in the shade and plopped down next to her friend.

"Got the kid again, huh?" Nancy peeled off a piece of red licorice and began to chew on it. "Want one?"

"I've got my Popsicle."

"It's dripping."

Lena gulped down the Popsicle in a few large bites and flung the two sticks into the trash can.

"Let's go over to my house," said Nancy. She lived on the top floor—the attic, really—of a red house two blocks away.

"I can't. I have Deedee. I bought some M&M's. Want some?" Lena pulled the package out of her pocket.

Nancy held out her hand and Lena poured the tiny colored candies over her palm.

The Pine brothers were riding their bikes through the park. Sam, the older one, zoomed toward the girls on stilts. One girl tottered and fell. The other girl jumped off and tried to jam one of her stilts into Sam's bike. Sam swerved away, laughing wildly.

Stewart, who was in Lena's grade, rode behind, watching his older brother. Stewart wore faded jeans and a red paisley cap, under which his face was thin and white, even at the end of summer. As he pedaled past Lena and Nancy, Lena pulled the carriage back from the sidewalk.

He passed without a threat or a word and disappeared under the elm trees, the sun and leaves making patterns of shadow and light on his back.

"Wouldn't you like to punch Sam Pine right in the nose?" Nancy said.

"What if he punched back?"

"Hit him again!"

"If he won, he'd brag to everyone."

"He wouldn't win. I'd make sure of that." Nancy dropped the last of the M&M's into her mouth and pulled another stick of licorice out of her pocket. "And when I finished with him, I'd flatten that Stewart."

"He never bothers anyone," said Lena. "It's always Sam."

"You like him?" Nancy asked slyly. "You've got a crush on Stewart Pine?"

"No!" Lena felt her face go hot. "Why would I like him, anyway? He gets all D's in school."

"The trouble with you Jewish people is that you're all brains and no muscles," Nancy said. "My mother said so."

Lena stared at her friend. Nancy was sitting in a patch of dirty grass, her strong arms and legs tanned and dusty. The licorice had stained her lips a purplish red. "You're crazy," Lena said.

"It's the truth." Nancy made the sign of the cross over her chest with a half-chewed piece of licorice. "I swear by the Father, the Son, and the Holy Ghost."

"Your mother's crazy, too," Lena added.

"But don't worry," Nancy continued. "At least you don't look Jewish. Not too much, anyway."

"Thanks a lot," said Lena. If her mother had overheard them, she would retort, "What are Jewish people *supposed* to look like?"

Nancy studied her for a moment. "You could almost be Italian. But not your father. Your father looks Irish."

Lena was slim, with blue eyes and straight black hair that she sometimes wore in braids; her father was tall and thin with curly red hair.

"Yeah," said Lena. "We're the only Irish-Italian-Jewish family on Moose Street."

"Hey, look at me!" Danette streaked past them on a pair of new white roller skates. "I'm the fastest skater on Moose Street!"

"There goes someone who could teach Sam Pine a lesson," said Nancy. "One that he'd never forget."

Danette had strong arms, a hard head, and she loved to fight. She had beaten up girls, boys, even a teenager once.

Lena tried to stay away from her. You didn't want to get on Danette's bad side.

The carriage creaked and stirred. "Mama?"

"Your kid is up," said Nancy.

Lena peered into the carriage. The baby had kicked off her blanket and thrown her toothbrush by her feet.

"Here's your toothbrush, Deedee," Lena said. Deedee carried the green toothbrush everywhere. She loved it more than her red-and-blue rattles, more than her windup tin monkey, more than the big white bear her uncle had given her last month.

"Does she ever let go of that thing?" Nancy said.

"Mama," Deedee said again.

"Mama's not here. Just Lena. Come to Lena."

"Gaga," said Deedee. Her plump body was warm and soft.

"Gaga," echoed Nancy. "Gaga, gaga, gaga."

Deedee held out her arms to Nancy. "Gaga."

"Gaga," Nancy repeated, taking the baby. "Don't you say anything else, kid?"

At the other end of the park a girl screamed.

Lena turned to see what was happening.

The group of teenage boys by the fountain was holding a girl by her arms and legs and swinging her over the brackish water.

"One! Two! Three!"

There was a tremendous splash and a shout of laughter.

The girl flailed in the foul green water.

"They're disgusting," said Nancy. She was holding Deedee on her lap and had given her a stick of licorice to chew on.

The girl climbed out of the fountain, her shorts and blouse clinging to her body.

"It's Roseanne!" Lena got to her feet and moved toward the fountain.

Roseanne was shaking her fist at the boys.

"Don't touch me! Don't touch me!" screeched one of them in mock terror.

Another boy held out his arms. "Kiss me, Roseanne. Your perfume is so sweet."

"Roseanne!" Lena called. "Are you all right?"

But the older girl had already run from the park.

"Roseanne!" the boys shouted mockingly. "Come back, Rosie, *please!*"

"Creeps," muttered Lena.

"Here's your sister." Nancy had come up behind her with Deedee over her shoulder, sucking on the green toothbrush. "You owe me half your wages," said Nancy. "I'm the one doing all the work. How much does your mother pay you, anyway?"

"Fifteen cents an hour."

"The kid weighs a ton. You ought to ask for twenty-five cents."

Lena held out her arms to her little sister. Deedee pointed to the swings. "Gaga," she said.

"She wants a ride," said Nancy. "You're going to have to do it. I'm going home."

"Sure," said Lena. "I'll see you later."

She glanced at the fountain. The teenage boys had disappeared. Stewart Pine was standing there now, his bike at his feet, his red cap pulled back on his head.

"Lena!" he called.

She lifted her hand in greeting.

"Catch this!" With one quick motion he took off the cap and spun it into the air.

It soared in a pure arc over the chalked sidewalk and curved toward Lena.

She reached out and caught it.

"It's yours!" Stewart called.

Lena put the hat on her head. It was a perfect fit.

The Gilly Sisters

"Do you think they're alive?" asked Nancy. She and Lena were sitting in the dark on the cold painted floor of Lena's room, staring at the lighted window across the yard.

Two bent, shadowy figures moved silently around a table in the room across the yard.

"They're ghosts."

"Really?" Nancy breathed.

"They never leave their house," whispered Lena. "But every night they walk back and forth, back and forth."

Next door to Lena lived two sisters whose name was Gilly. She had to pass their house every day on the way to and from school. It was a small dark red house with a screened-in porch.

Walking by, Lena could never resist a quick glance at the house. Sometimes she saw pale faces behind a heavy screen. Sometimes she heard muttering voices, the squeak of a rocker, and the scrape of chair legs. Lena always forced herself to walk slowly past the Gilly sisters' house, but as soon as she reached the edge of their lawn, she broke into a run.

Sometimes when she was playing she was suddenly aware of the sisters. When she lifted Deedee up and twirled her around at the side of the house, or when she pretended to chase her through the yard, she somehow knew that the two sisters had put down their crocheting and swiveled around in their rocking chairs so that they faced the Rosens' yard.

"They're carrying something," said Nancy.

"Heads of dead people," Lena said.

Nancy shuddered deliciously.

"They have lived for hundreds of years, eating only dead blackbirds. Every night strange howling sounds come from inside their house—"

"Sssh!" said Nancy. "They're watching!"

One of the old women had come to the window. She stood for a moment looking out, a dim figure with rough unruly hair.

"She's looking at us!"

The old woman was staring directly at the girls. They dove to the floor.

"Do you think she saw?"

"She wants to put our heads on a platter," said Lena. The two girls laughed nervously.

"I hope she didn't see us watching," said Lena. "I have to go by her house every day."

"You said she doesn't leave her house."

"Well, she sits on her porch a lot. But she

never walks out the door. Even though she's my next-door neighbor, I've never seen her face—or her sister's."

"You've lived here six years and you've never seen her face?"

"Not up close," said Lena. "Across the yard or from behind a screen. And that's as close as I want to get!"

The girls lifted their heads above the sill. The curtain was drawn now. The window across the driveway was closed and dark.

"I'm going over to the Gillys'," Lena's mother announced one day.

"Why?" Lena asked.

"Florence Gilly had the flu last week. The changing seasons, she told me." Her mother wrapped a meat loaf and a plate of cookies, and put on her brown dress with the yellow collar. "You're in charge, Lena," she called as she went out the door.

Lena read to Deedee, played spider with

her, read some more. They went up the stairs to their uncle's apartment, but he wasn't home, so they came back down. Why couldn't her mother let the Gilly sisters take care of themselves? One hour and she still wasn't back. What was she doing over there? Why did it take so long? What did they need from her mother, anyway?

Lena got Deedee's bottle out of the refrigerator and propped it up in the baby's hands. The Gilly sisters were probably making their report. They were telling her mother how Lena watched them at night from her darkened room.

Or maybe they had given Lena's mother a poison powder. Or had stuck tiny needles in her arms that would put her to sleep. Tonight Lena would look across the yard and it would be her mother's head that lay on the platter. . . .

"Daaat!" screamed Deedee. The bottle had

fallen out of her small chubby hands. "Daaat, daat!"

"Oh, *here,* baby. Now hold on to it."

Lena heard footsteps in the hallway. Her mother came in holding an empty plate.

Lena scanned her mother's face anxiously—it was the same, no poisonous tint or deadly pallor. And her arms and legs were in all the right places.

"Would you believe they keep that house in perfect order?" Lena's mother asked. "Two old ladies and not a speck of dust."

"You were gone so *long.*"

"They're just getting their strength back," her mother said. "There's nothing in their refrigerator. I'm sending you over tomorrow with a pot of soup."

No! thought Lena. Never! But she couldn't say that to her mother. Her mother would smile at her fears, give her a little encouraging pat on the back, and send her along. Not knowing that she was sending her oldest daughter into a deadly trap. . . .

Lena walked slowly up the immaculate stairs holding a large pot of soup that was still warm.

From inside the darkened porch she could hear the creak of two rocking chairs. "Don't dawdle, child."

Lena pulled open the screen door. The odor of stale violets and shuttered rooms greeted her.

"Sit down," said a different voice, soft but a little more clipped.

"Yes, Miss Gilly."

The sisters were sitting in painted rocking chairs. Lena lifted her eyes and saw long white hands with blue veins crocheting beige doilies.

"Do you crochet, dear?" The soft voice belonged to a shapeless dress with some kind of sprawling pink flower like a cabbage.

"No, Miss Gilly."

"Knit?" asked the other one, who was wearing a blue cotton housedress. She had pale thin legs ending in stiff leather shoes.

"No, Miss Gilly."

"I suppose you might sew some of your own clothes then, a big girl like you."

"No, Miss Gilly."

"No?" The sister in the flowered dress sounded shocked. Was she the younger one?

"Your mother was here yesterday," said the blue-dress sister.

Lena held out the pot of soup. "This is for you. My mother sent it."

"How very Christian of her," said the younger sister in her soft voice.

"Put it here on the table," said the other sister.

Keeping her eyes fixed on the lid of the pot, Lena placed it on the table and quickly sat down again.

"Have a cookie," said the blue-dress sister—the elder? She held out a plate, and Lena gingerly took a small cookie. It was dry and hard, with a strange smell as though it had been stored in a drawer with mothballs.

"Good, isn't it?"

Lena nodded and crumbled the cookie in her hand, letting it trickle into her pocket.

"Have another."

"Thank you, Miss Gilly." She took another cookie and held it in her lap. "I'll keep this one for my sister."

"She has good manners," said the elder sister. "A good girl."

"A good girl," repeated the younger.

Lena raised her eyes a few inches to the elaborate fringes of crocheted brown shawls. "Do you ever need any errands done?" she asked. "I could go to the store for you sometime."

"How very kind of you, dear."

"The store delivers to our house."

"You're a very thoughtful little girl."

"Do you fight with your sister?" asked the elder one. Her hands were whirling the beige yarn and the crochet hook at high speed.

"No, Miss Gilly," said Lena. She stared at the thin white ankles.

"Of course she doesn't," said the younger. "She's not that kind of girl."

"I hope not," said the elder. "Did you hear about the little boy who hit his sister with a brick?"

Lena shook her head.

"She foamed at the mouth and then died," the elder sister said.

"Wasn't it a shame," said the younger sister.

"Don't ever hit your sister with a brick," said the elder.

"She wouldn't do that," murmured the younger.

"And don't put pillows over her face, either."

"Or hold her head under water."

"Don't wind cords around her neck."

"Or put rat poison in her cup."

Lena raised her eyes and stared at the two sisters rocking on their green chairs. Their faces were soft and plump. The elder sister worked her yarn. The younger sister had folded her puffy bluish hands over the needlework on her lap and was smiling into the distance.

"Don't ever do that," said the Gilly sisters together. "Don't ever do that."

It is midnight. Lena and Nancy lie facing each other on the floor of Lena's room, each curled inside a musty-smelling green sleeping bag.

"Tell me more," whispers Nancy.

"It is late at night," Lena says in a hoarse whisper. "All the lights are out in the young girl's house. She crouches by her bedroom window gazing across the yard, where a light shines from behind gauzy curtains. A shadowy bent figure comes to the window. An old woman gazes at the girl's house, straight at her. Although the light is dim, the girl can see the woman's face quite clearly. It is soft and plump and empty."

Clutching her pillow, Nancy stares at Lena, her mouth slightly open.

Underneath them the furnace comes on with a roar. Both girls jump.

"What's that?" Nancy says.

Lena shivers. She knows it's just the furnace, but the floor still shakes, and it's a moment before she can speak again.

"The woman's mouth moves silently," Lena says.

" 'Don't ever do that,' she says. 'Don't ever do that.' "

Stealing

Lena rang the doorbell of the blue house at the far end of Moose Street and plucked the top box off the pile of square white boxes she was carrying.

A heavyset man came to the door. "Yes? What can I do for you, miss?"

"Good afternoon," Lena began politely as she had been taught. She held the open box up to him. "Would you like to buy some greeting cards?"

The big man took the box of cards from Lena and thumbed through them. "Not today, miss. Sorry."

"Another time?" Lena asked. The little green booklet that had come with the boxes of cards had told her to say this whenever she failed to make a sale.

"Maybe." He closed the door.

Lena sighed, adjusted the pile of boxes under her arm, and set off down Moose Street.

The cards had glittery pictures of blue birds and pink skies and yellow flowers on the front and sentimental messages written in gold script on the inside. They weren't selling very well. Lena had been going door to door for two and a half hours now and had found only three buyers. Her uncle had taken one box, Nancy's mother, another, and she had sold one to rabbity Mr. Catalano at the candy store.

"Be sure to go to the Gillys," her mother had said as Lena left the house.

"Never," Lena had answered when her mother was out of earshot.

She wasn't that desperate for a sale.

She had first seen the advertisement on the

back of a comic book: EARN MONEY IN YOUR
SPARE TIME. NO INVESTMENT REQUIRED. YOUR
NEIGHBORS WILL LOVE OUR ATTRACTIVE AS-
SORTMENT OF GREETING CARDS.

The cards cost a dollar fifty for a box of
twenty-four cards. Lena would get to keep a
quarter for every box she sold.

If she sold twenty boxes of cards—surely
that would be easy on Moose Street—she
would earn five dollars. The more boxes she
sold, the more money they would pay her. If
she sold forty boxes, she would earn twelve
dollars. . . .

The boxes of cards had arrived in a big
carton yesterday.

"Hey, Lena!" In a grubby jacket and old
jeans, Stewart Pine was sitting on the Methodist church stairs, bouncing a ball. "What
are you doing?"

"I'm selling cards," said Lena.

"Let me see." Stewart pulled out a box.
"Very nice. I'll buy some."

"They're a dollar fifty . . ."

He waved her away. "Oh, that's nothing."

"Do you send a lot of cards?"

"I will now," said Stewart. He pulled six quarters from his jeans pocket and held them out in his open palm.

"Do you want the all-occasion assortment?" asked Lena.

"Yeah, sure."

Stewart pointed to Lena's cap. "Nice hat," he said.

It was the red paisley cap he had tossed to her in the park.

"Yes," said Lena shyly.

They started walking up the street together, Lena with the boxes of cards under her arm, Stewart whistling a tune.

"Have you sold a lot of cards?"

"Just a few."

"What are you going to buy with the money?"

"A new pair of roller skates."

They turned a corner.

"I live over there." Stewart pointed to an unpainted two-story house behind a motorcycle shop.

"Wait here," he said, and ran up the steps.

The yard was filled with rusting bikes and piles of tires. Some of the windows had cardboard and sheets of plastic taped over them. Three shirts hung from a clothesline.

Screams and shouts came from the house. Then a crash.

Should I leave? Lena wondered. Should I go home?

The door opened and Stewart stumbled out. One cheek was blazing red, but he smiled at Lena.

"I'm going to the P and C," he said as though nothing had happened. "Do you want to come with me?"

Lena hesitated.

"You might sell some cards there."

"Okay . . . I guess."

They turned onto North Main Street, past the funeral parlor and the music shop, past the convent and the ice cream store.

Stewart grabbed her arm. "There's my stepfather," he said. He steered her into the music shop so fast that Lena only caught a glimpse of a short red-faced man in a gray mechanic's suit.

She found herself among organs, pianos, accordians, and guitars. Stewart walked from keyboard to keyboard, tapping out a few notes here, a few notes there.

"Do you play?" Lena asked Stewart.

"What do you want, children?" A tall woman, almost a giant, with deep curved shadows under her eyes, stepped out from a door at the back.

Lena shifted the boxes of cards under her arm. "Would you . . ." she began. "Would you like—"

"What we would like," Stewart interrupted, "is to know about guitar lessons."

"Guitar lessons?" The woman looked from Stewart to Lena, taking in the dirty jacket, the old jeans, and the boxes of cards. "How many years have you played?"

"None," stammered Lena.

"Five," said Stewart. "My teacher told me I'm getting too good for her. She told me to come here."

Lena thought that Stewart was growing larger as she watched him. Soon he would be taller than the giant woman. Soon he would fill the music shop.

The woman smiled, disappeared behind a counter, and came back with a card. "Here you go, young man. Here are our rates and hours for advanced lessons. You can call this number to make arrangements."

"Thank you very much." Stewart half-bowed, as though to a large and important audience. "I will be in touch." He nodded to Lena. "Time to go home."

"Yes," whispered Lena.

But Stewart's stepfather was waiting outside the store, his arms folded across his chest. His face was red and swollen. "Well?" he demanded of Stewart. "What were you doing in that store?"

"Lena wanted to see about guitar lessons," Stewart said. "She's been studying for five years."

"Do you always follow girls around? Won't the boys play with you?"

"I have to go to the P and C," Stewart said. "Mom wants me to get some milk."

The man jabbed his finger in the air. "Don't change the subject. You're supposed to be home doing chores."

"Mom sent me." Stewart's voice rose slightly. "She needs some milk. She sent me to the store."

"You better not be lying, boy!"

Stewart and Lena continued silently down North Main.

At the store Stewart held the door open

for Lena. She followed him to the cooler, where he took a carton of milk from the shelf.

Stewart had a weird smile on his face that made Lena feel both afraid and excited. He gestured for her to follow him and led her down another aisle.

They stood in front of shelves of stationery. Fat pink erasers, little brown notebooks, smooth wooden rulers . . .

Stewart looked quickly around and grabbed a handful of erasers and a notebook, which he stuffed into his pocket. His eyes were intense, almost harsh. He motioned to Lena.

She hesitated, then met his gaze . . . and wrapped her fingers around a small brown notebook.

The cashier seemed to take forever to put the quart of milk in a brown paper bag. Finally she handed it to Stewart and he and Lena walked quickly toward the door.

"Young man!" called the cashier just as Lena pushed open the door. "Young man, come back here!"

Lena froze. She thought she would faint with fear. Stewart gave her a little shove. Go on, get out, he said with his eyes. She began to move forward. Her legs were shaking. The greeting cards were falling out of her arms.

Outside, through the large glass windows, Lena saw the cashier taking everything out of Stewart's pockets. The box of cards he had bought from her lay open by the cash register. Lena saw Stewart talking, shrugging, falling silent.

She touched the notebook in her pocket and waited for Stewart to turn around and point to her. Should she run? But Stewart did not point to her. What was going to happen to him? Lena shivered in the chilly air. But she did not leave. She would stay until the end.

The cashier had made Stewart take off his

jacket, and as he stood in the store in his shirt sleeves with all his pockets emptied he looked strangely beautiful. He had nothing left now; everything had been taken away. There was only Lena waiting on the sidewalk.

The Blizzard

"I'm going to beat you up," Danette told Lena one bleak November day in school.

Lena pretended not to hear.

"Tonight after school. You'll get what's coming to you."

Maybe if she acted as if she didn't hear, it wouldn't be real.

"I'll be waiting for you." Danette walked away.

Lena couldn't contain herself anymore. "Why? What did I do to you?" she called after Danette.

Danette didn't turn around.

Lena hated to fight, and she never did. She knew she would be a pushover in a fight. She would go down like a deck of cards.

"Why does she want to beat you up?" Nancy asked. "What did you do to her?"

"I don't know!" Lena said.

Had Lena laughed at a joke she shouldn't have? Had she looked at Arthur the wrong way? (Everyone knew he was Danette's. He was the smartest boy in the fifth grade—quiet, handsome, never in trouble. But no girl in her right mind would talk to him without Danette's permission.)

Maybe Danette didn't like the way Lena talked or answered questions in class. Maybe she didn't like the color of her shoes or the way she drew.

"There's no reason," Lena told Nancy. "She just wants to beat me up."

Lena knew that Danette would clobber her.

Danette would punch her, pinch her, tear her clothes, and pull her hair.

The loss of dignity seemed the worst: boys and girls circling the fighting pair, cheering them, jeering them, watching Lena get beaten, humiliated, crushed into nothing.

There was no way to stop it.

She couldn't call her mother or father. She couldn't tell the teachers. Only crybabies or tattletales did that—even Danette would never do something that despicable.

Would Stewart protect her? He hadn't been in school for more than a week. Miss Fulman had said he was sick with the flu. Sick or well, Lena knew that Danette would make mincemeat out of Stewart in five minutes flat.

Lena couldn't apologize; she didn't know what she had done. For one moment she desperately wished she had subscribed to one of those judo-by-mail courses advertised on the backs of comic books. Too late.

She would have to either face Danette or outsmart her.

That afternoon Lena made herself extra helpful to Miss Fulman. She washed the blackboard. She cleaned the erasers. She handed out papers and wrote homework assignments on the board. And when the school bell rang to dismiss the students from class, she went up to the teacher.

"Could I walk out with you?" she asked.

Miss Fulman looked up, her thin dry hands resting on a pile of books and papers. She had been teaching at Moose Street School for forty years. Had she been young and vigorous once? Lena imagined her shrinking with every class she taught, until she had become tiny and creased like a withered apple.

"Why, of course, Lena."

The teacher put on her heavy winter coat and black galoshes, tied a blue scarf with white snowflakes around her neck, and gathered a pile of books and papers from her desk. "Let's go now."

Danette and a group of girls and boys were huddled in a tight circle by the outside stairs.

They had been waiting for her.

"Good night, boys and girls." Miss Fulman gave them her tight, withered smile.

"Good night, Miss Fulman."

"Catch you later, Lena," said Danette.

Lena hugged her books to her chest and pretended that she hadn't heard.

The sound of laughter followed Lena and the teacher as they made their way through the schoolyard toward Moose Street.

"Whatever do they find to laugh about?" Miss Fulman asked.

Lena shrugged.

When they got to Moose Street, she paused. "Good-bye, Miss Fulman."

"Good night, Lena."

There was no sign of Danette or her friends. But Lena ran all the way home.

The next afternoon, Tuesday, everyone had religious education. Danette was at church, and Lena walked home alone.

On the third afternoon Danette was waiting by the stairs when Lena came out, but so was Lena's uncle. He sometimes took a walk in the late afternoon, picked up a bag of candy at Catalano's, and swung around to the school to meet Lena. Lena's heart leaped when she saw his red and orange jacket like a beacon in the crowd of boys and girls outside the door.

"I was out and thought I'd come meet you," he said, stubbing out his cigar on the concrete steps.

Danette glared at Lena as if to say, "You won't get away from me much longer." Lena took her uncle's arm.

On the fourth afternoon Lena and Nancy got out a few minutes ahead of the rest of the class and made a dash for it. They wriggled under a gate, hauled themselves over a picket fence, trampled a few dead flower stalks, and smudged their coats as they squeezed between two garages.

"There has got to be a better way," panted Nancy as they landed safely in Lena's yard. "Why don't you fight her and get it over with?"

"I can't!" wailed Lena. "You know I can't. She'll kill me."

"You can't avoid her forever. Sooner or later she's going to get you."

"Well, what would you do?"

"I wouldn't fight her either," admitted Nancy.

On the fifth day, a dreary Friday, it began to snow.

It snowed all morning while they sat in the darkening classroom reading their social studies book and writing lists of spelling words.

It snowed while they ate lunch and when they lined up to go back to their classroom.

At two o'clock Miss Fulman clapped her thin hands together. "School is dismissed early today because of the weather," she announced. "Get your coats and boots and hats."

Lena's stomach gave a little lurch. There would be no running from Danette in this snow. She hadn't even worn boots this morning. And now she was going to get her face rubbed in the snow, have cold wet lumps of ice dropped down her back, and stinging snowballs thrown at her on the way home.

Gathering up her books, she got her coat and hat and scarf and walked slowly down the hallway toward the front door. Maybe if she didn't fight back, Danette would give up after a few punches.

Could she faint, fake a fit, throw up?

Maybe someone would come to her rescue. But who? Who was brave enough to face Danette?

"You are going to get killed," Lena said to herself for about the thousandth time that week.

The schoolyard was empty. Only hundreds of footprints ran through the snow toward Moose Street.

Danette, Arthur, the twins, Nancy— everyone was gone. And Lena had been forgotten.

The snow, the snow, the wonderful snow had come to rescue her!

Her shoes were soaked and the snow clung to her bare legs and dripped down her socks in icy lumps, but Lena was happy.

"It's snowing!" Lena called joyously to her father, who was shoveling the porch steps.

"It's snowing!" Lena announced to her mother as she ran into the house, her arms loaded with schoolbooks.

Deedee tottered into the living room like a little windup toy. She pulled herself up to the window and pointed outside. "Ssss, sss, ss," she said, wrinkling her nose and toppling onto her mother's legs.

It snowed while Lena did her math homework, folded the laundry, played with Deedee, and ate her supper. It snowed while she washed, dried, and put away the dishes.

It snowed when she called Nancy on the phone, and it snowed when Mary Catherine called to ask about the social studies homework.

It was still snowing when Lena put on her blue flannel pajamas. It snowed while she stood over the heating vent and let the warm air blow up her pajama legs, puff out her hair, and rush over her face. It snowed when she climbed into her cold white bed and turned off the light.

On Saturday it snowed the entire day. She stood at the window and watched the snowflakes plummet to the ground. They slid down the roofs of Moose Street houses and collected in the drainpipes. They frosted tree branches and wooden fences, coated the sidewalks of Moose Street, and fell thickly on the road so that cars skidded and slid when they turned the corner.

Across the yard at the Gilly sisters' house, Lena saw two ghostly figures moving silently behind a veil of snow.

She stayed in her room all day Sunday making clay igloos, men with baskets of fish, and fat women hunched over fires. She imagined the snow going on forever, blanketing and protecting her. She would be sealed in a magical world of purest white where no one could ever reach her.

On Monday factories were closed, stores were closed, schools were closed.

When Lena got up on Tuesday morning, the snow had stopped. The world was white and flawless.

All was silent. No motors revving, no factory whistles, no chained wheels grinding over snow. Not even the sound of a snowplow. Lena heard only a faint muffled scratching as the first shovels began to dig out the buried houses of Moose Street.

After breakfast, she dressed in her warmest clothing. There were two of everything: sweaters, socks, mittens. She pulled plastic bags over her socks and fastened them at the ankles with rubber bands. Boots were shoved over the bags, and finally, a long green scarf was wound around her neck and face so that only her eyes were showing.

She was ready.

The deep perfect snow awaited her.

It lay over the porch like a wave of marble.

Lena walked slowly to the edge of the porch, watching her footsteps and the icy blue shadows they left. Then she let herself fall, fall into mounds of soft cold snow. It felt like feathers under her arms and legs. It felt as though she were being buried in glittering frozen goose down.

The front door opened. "Here we are," said Lena's father. His red hair stuck out under a bright blue cap. He had one shovel over his shoulder and another under his arm. Her uncle followed in his red and orange hunting jacket.

"Catch," said her father. He threw her a shovel. The three of them shoveled. They shoveled until they could walk from the porch to the sidewalk, and then from the sidewalk to the neighbors'. And each neighbor linked their cleared sidewalk to the next, until Lena could walk from her house to the school to the park, and even as far as Miss Fulman's house at the other end of Moose Street.

Lena lumbered up the street until she met Nancy and the twins.

"Let's make a snowman!" said Mary Catherine and Catherine Mary.

"I'll make the head!" Lena took a snowball and began to roll it in the snow.

"Lena!" Nancy said. "Here comes Danette."

Arthur was pulling Danette on a sled down the middle of Moose Street. She wore a bright blue parka with fur around the collar. Her cheeks were red and little flakes of white snow clung to her curly hair.

"Here!" called the twins. "Help us make this snowman!"

Danette's black eyes darted back and forth, resting for a moment on Lena.

Lena's heart began to thud. She moved her snowball away from Danette, rolling it over and over in the snow. If only she could roll it over Danette.

Arthur was helping Danette out of the sled.

Lena thought of running away. But she had done enough of that. She wouldn't run and she couldn't fight.

54

Danette popped a red gumdrop into her mouth. "Where's the head?" she said.

Lena rolled the snowman's head slowly toward Danette.

Danette dropped another gumdrop into her mouth.

Lena knelt down, picked up the great snowball she had made, and dropped it on top of the snowman's body.

"That head is crooked," said Danette.

Slowly Lena unwound her green scarf and draped it over the snowman's shoulders.

Danette's lip curled. "You're supposed to *tie* it."

Lena felt in her pockets and pulled out a couple of chestnuts, shined them on her coat, and then carefully put them on the snowman's face for eyes.

"That looks dumb without a mouth."

"Well, give it one, then," said Lena.

Danette scowled at Lena.

"C'mon, Danette, give it a mouth," said Nancy. "Be a sport!"

"Yes," said Mary Catherine and Catherine Mary. "Give it a mouth, Danette!"

Danette glared at her friends, then pulled out a handful of gumdrops and shoved them into the snowman's face. "I hope everyone is happy now!"

Lena knelt down in the snow and began to roll another snowball. She glanced over at Danette. Then she looked at the snowman with its chestnut eyes and crooked gumdrop mouth. The mouth seemed to frown at her, as though it did not want to be on the snowman's face.

Lena wanted to straighten that mouth, to make it smile pleasantly at her. But she didn't dare. Not with Danette watching.

Still, the mouth was on the snowman's face—and Danette had put it there.

Danette would not bother her again today, Lena knew, and perhaps not for a long time.

She gave her snowball a little push and zigzagged it down a slope.

"Come on, everybody," Lena called. "Let's make another snowman!"

Religious Education

When people ask Lena her religion, she gets dizzy. Her face gets hot. She stares at the sidewalk.

Religion is important on Moose Street. Are you a Catholic, or are you a Protestant? Methodist or Presbyterian? Which church do you go to? Lena is neither a Catholic nor a Protestant. She does not go to a church. She is Jewish. From one end of Moose Street to another, for five square miles of solid houses in any direction, there are no Jewish families. Except for Lena's.

Lena brings out the words slowly, in a low

voice, as if she hopes the words might fly away on a gust of wind before they are heard. But the words always hover in the air right in front of her, too clear and too loud. "I'm Jewish."

"Jewish?"

"What's that?"

"You're one of those."

"Are you an Indian?"

"You're the ones who killed Christ."

"Is that why you wear pigtails?"

Sometimes she tries to explain in the careful sentences that her mother has taught her. "Christ was a Jew."

"No, he was a Christian."

"The first Christian," says Lena. "He was born a Jew."

"How come the Jews killed him?"

"The Romans killed him."

"The Jews did."

"No, they didn't!"

"Yes, they did!"

It is a bother, a burden to be Jewish and always have to defend yourself.

It is spring now, and on Sunday mornings the Rosen family works outside. Lena's father rakes leaves or trims dead branches from the trees. Lena's mother transplants flowers, digs new beds, prunes bushes. Deedee sprinkles dirt on her head. And Lena's uncle sits on the porch and smokes a cigar.

When the church-bound procession of well-scrubbed faces, crisply ironed dresses, and suits and elegant hats of all colors passes by the Rosens' house, Lena is on her hands and knees weeding. It's precisely ten to nine in the morning. The bells for early mass have rung long ago, and the solitary devout worshippers have gone home. Now flocks of parents, children, grandparents, and cousins walk proudly toward St. Mary's or toward the Methodist and Presbyterian churches.

The twins, Mary Catherine and Catherine Mary, waltz by with arms linked. They wear shiny patent leather shoes, pink and yellow flowered dresses with large sashes and starched petticoats. The twins are always clean and shining. "Hello, Lena!" they call.

A few minutes later Nancy comes past in a plain red dress with a navy collar. Her blond hair is set in tight little curls under a small navy straw hat.

Nancy walks fast with her head down. Her mother is behind her, waving to all the neighbors and shouting out greetings. When Nancy sees Lena, she stops and smiles. "See you after church," she says.

"Hey, kid!" calls Roseanne, Lena's old baby-sitter, resplendent in a yellow dress and shiny yellow pumps. Her thick hair is teased at the top, and she wears pale pink lipstick and blue eye shadow.

Then comes Danette, walking like a majorette on parade, magnificent in a bright blue cotton dress with matching leather purse and low-heeled shoes. Danette stares straight ahead without even glancing at the Rosens, her round face full of piety and holy scorn.

Sometimes Arthur also walks past the Rosens' house. Five brothers and two sisters follow him. If he's not busy with little brothers or sisters, Arthur nods to Lena and her parents.

When Arthur strolls down Moose Street, Danette lingers at the corner until he catches up to her.

On her hands and knees in the dirt, Lena mumbles hello to the twins and Nancy. She half-smiles at Arthur. She ignores Danette as much as she can. She is sure that all the neighbors are staring at her family with their rocks and rakes and dirt-smeared clothes. And she feels ashamed—of herself and her religion, which is somehow to blame for this weekly humiliation. Why isn't she like everyone else? Why does her family always have to be different?

In school all the students—except Lena—

attend religious education once a week at a neighborhood church. At the beginning of the year each boy or girl brings home a green printed card on which the parents check off religion and church and sign their permission for weekly religious instruction.

These green cards have no listing for a synagogue. There is no listing for "Religion: Jewish." Lena's parents must write a special note on the bottom of the card, asking for her to be excused because she is Jewish and there is no nearby synagogue.

On Tuesday afternoons everyone is dismissed two hours early. The boys and girls line up and walk in single file out of the classroom, down the hall, across the schoolyard, and along the sidewalks of Moose Street. Lena stays at her desk and watches them go.

She sits in the empty silent schoolroom and does her homework. If she has finished her homework, she is allowed to read a book. The teachers are kind, terribly kind. Lena is the only Jewish person ever to attend Moose Street School.

Sometimes Miss Fulman talks to her and asks her questions about her religion.

Lena tells Miss Fulman about the eight days of Hanukkah, about menorahs and spinning tops called dreidels. She talks about Purim and Queen Esther, who saved the Jews through her beauty and wit.

Miss Fulman is pleased. She tells Lena what a bright, well-behaved girl she is. Her parents should be proud. The other students should consider themselves lucky. She is a credit to her religion.

The Rosens are not a religious family. They never attend synagogue, not even on the High Holy days. They don't observe the Sabbath. They barely celebrate the holidays. Hanukkah and Passover, that's about it.

Lena doesn't even know any other Jewish people, except for her cousins in New York, whom she visits once a year.

What Lena knows about her religion comes from large heavy books, full of old photographs and stories of martyrdom and persecution, as well as stories of scientific, legal, or artistic genius. She reads Anne Frank's diary. She reads about ghettos, pogroms, inquisitions, and concentration camps. She reads about Moses and Einstein and Spinoza, about the Gershwins and Copeland and Freud.

Sometimes her uncle tells her a story or two—about the Maccabees, or Lot's wife and the pillar of salt, or about Jacob and his ladder.

Lena is really "not very Jewish at all." That's what strangers say when they meet her. That's what her cousins say when she visits them during the holidays. Even her uncle says it from time to time.

Lena has no wish to be very Jewish. She does not want to light candles on Friday night, to eat milk and meat separately, to go without electricity on the Sabbath like her religious New York cousins. She does not want to go to the synagogue on the other side of the city and sit in marble pews with other Jewish girls and boys and sing songs.

Sometimes she wonders if she is really Jewish.

One day the twins decide to baptize Lena.

They are dressed in crisp red and white dresses, each with a small gold cross at her neck.

"The Jews killed Christ, you know." Mary Catherine looks at Lena accusingly.

"I didn't do it," Lena says. One thousand nine hundred thirty years later, the guilt of Christ's death in Palestine has come through the centuries to attach itself to her, Lena Rosen, ankle deep in a pile of last fall's withered leaves in a Moose Street backyard.

Mary Catherine stands close to her. "If you die without being baptized, you'll go to hell."

The twins have large wooden crosses above their beds and pictures of Jesus by their dressers. The twins drop candy in the dirt, make the sign of the cross over it, and pop it into their mouths. The twins steal and lie and say bad words. Then they go to confession and their souls are spotless again.

"I don't believe in hell." Lena wonders why she has to suffer for a religion that she doesn't practice or even believe in.

"Go get the holy water," Mary Catherine says to her sister.

"I don't want to be baptized."

"Or else you'll go to purgatory," says Mary Catherine. "That's where all the dead babies go."

The two sisters crowd Lena. "We just want to save your soul."

"*We* are going to heaven twice as fast," says Mary Catherine, "because there are two of us."

Catherine Mary scoops up some water that has collected in a drainpipe along with some soggy fall leaves. "In the name of the Father, the Son, and the Holy Ghost . . ." She flings a handful of water at Lena's face.

"Now make the sign of the cross," says Mary Catherine.

"We've saved your soul," says Catherine Mary.

A vision of centuries of martyred Jews—of men and women who have suffered for their religion—flashes through Lena's mind. She rubs her face with her sleeve. She is now one of them.

Blue Sky, No Rocket

On the day the astronauts went into space Lena and her classmates had art class. Miss Woodhead was the art teacher at Moose Street School. She was neither young nor old, neither ugly nor pretty. She was medium height, medium weight, medium age. Each week Miss Woodhead handed out paper and crayons to the class. They drew. Sometimes they painted.

"We are going to draw rockets today," Miss Woodhead announced. "We are going to draw the astronauts going into space."

Danette waved her hand. "I saw the rocket on television this morning, Miss Woodhead."

"So did I!" called Stewart Pine.

"Raise your hand," said Miss Woodhead. "Don't speak out of turn."

Mary Catherine said, "We saw pictures in a magazine."

"Very good," said the teacher. She handed everyone a large white sheet of paper and a set of crayons.

"Now I want you all to draw pictures of the rocket," she instructed the class. "Then we will put them up on the walls."

Lena looked at the paper. She looked at the crayons. She looked at Miss Woodhead, who was sitting at her desk making notes on a piece of paper.

When Lena was home, sitting at the kitchen table, she drew black snowflakes, green tulips, and blue leaves. She made red skies and orange grass. She drew giant people and tiny houses and floating castles with invisible princesses.

But at school it was pumpkins and turkeys, pilgrims and witches in the fall.

In the winter it was snowmen, snowflakes, sleds, stars, and Christmas trees.

Skies were always blue. Grass was always green. Flowers were always red and yellow. Children always smiled. And no one ever colored out of the lines.

Now Lena looked around at what the other boys and girls were doing.

Danette was drawing a fat silver rocket with plump smiling astronauts waving to the people below.

Stewart was drawing a skinny gray rocket that looked like a bullet with a huge jet of flame at its base.

Nancy's rocket was as big as the page.

For a moment Lena hesitated. Then she picked up her crayon and began to sketch the outline of a woman's head. She drew long black curls, then large blue eyes. The woman was carrying a book and wore high heels. The rocket could come later, Lena thought. Now she wanted to draw people.

Soon Lena had forgotten about the classroom, had forgotten about Miss Woodhead. Nothing existed except the page that she filled with people, who each had a separate name and personality. They were walking along a road with their heads tilted at odd angles, looking at something that was not on the page, something far away and in the sky.

"Time to put down your crayons," called Miss Woodhead.

Lena slowly looked up from her picture.

"What's *that*?" asked Mary Catherine, looking at Lena's paper.

Mary Catherine had drawn a watery sky and a bright sun. Catherine Mary had drawn a night sky full of pointed yellow stars. They had both drawn sleek, streamlined rockets.

"Where are your astronauts?" asked Catherine Mary.

"You're going to get in trouble," Mary Catherine said.

"Quiet, children!" Miss Woodhead walked along the aisles, red pen in hand, marking the pictures.

"Excellent work," she said to Danette. She wrote a large A plus in red ink at the top of the picture. Danette beamed.

"Very nice, Mary Catherine. Good work, Catherine Mary." The twins each got an A minus.

She even put a large B plus on Stewart Pine's picture. "Better than usual," Miss Woodhead said.

Esther Brown got a C. "Your rocket is too small." Some of the kids snickered.

And Nancy got a B minus. "Your rocket

is too big." Nancy shrugged. She didn't like art anyway.

"And Lena . . ." Miss Woodhead moved down the aisle toward Lena.

Lena looked up.

"Where's your rocket?" Miss Woodhead said. "This is not what I asked you to do!"

"They're going to the rocket launch," said Lena.

"Yes," said Nancy. "They're on their way to see the rocket."

Miss Woodhead wrote a large D minus on the paper.

The class was silent. "I saw the traffic jams on television this morning," Lena explained. "All the people got out of their cars to look at the sky."

The teacher turned away. "Everyone pass your pictures to the front. Danette, Mary Catherine, Catherine Mary, and Stewart, put up the work."

Her face hot, Lena watched as the pictures were taped to the walls.

Miss Woodhead looked at the clock. "Class dismissed," she said. "Back to your regular classroom."

"Ha, ha," said Danette. As she passed Lena she struck out with her foot and caught Lena on the ankle.

Lena looked straight ahead and pretended she didn't feel it.

"Come on, Lena!" said Nancy.

But Lena didn't move.

"Don't listen to old Woodhead," whispered Nancy. "She's solid from ear to ear."

Lena stared at the pictures. Silver shining rockets burst forth from every page. Twenty-four students in the class. And twenty-three pictures of shiny, cone-shaped rockets with swirls of red fire. Some of the pictures showed the sun. Others showed the moon.

Hers was the only empty sky in sight. And

yet something about that empty sky pleased her, filled her.

"What does she know," Lena said to herself fiercely. "The rocket is there. She just couldn't see it."

Birthday Party

Lena stood before the big mirror in the bath-room. Everything was perfect, perfect, from the white headband to the shiny patent leather shoes with the ballerina straps. The red party dress with puffed sleeves and a white collar, the big sash her mother had tied in a bow, the charm bracelet with the tiny golden sleds, skates, and bicycle on her wrist—it was all perfect.

She had been hearing about the party for weeks—the cake, the favors, the games. It was going to be the grandest and the biggest party of the year, held the week before school let out. Mary Catherine and Catherine Mary were turning eleven and Miss Fulman's entire fifth-grade class had been invited to their house this Saturday—from Danette to Nancy to Stewart to Lena. Even dumpy Esther Brown had gotten an invitation, though she was not coming, of course. She wouldn't dare.

"Here's the twins' present," said Lena's mother. She gave Lena a square package wrapped in blue with a big yellow ribbon on top. It was a violet book of fairy tales—one of Lena's favorites. Her mother had taken her downtown to the bookstore to buy it.

Lena skipped across the room. Her hair swung softly around her face. Her full red skirt bounced and swirled and rustled. She felt very grown up.

"Good-bye, Mother. Good-bye, Father."

"Have a good time," said her father. "Don't eat too much cake."

"Remember to thank the twins' parents!"

called her mother as Lena hurried out the door with the present under her arm.

The twins lived only a few blocks away in one of the big houses on Moose Street. Lena climbed the brick steps and rang the doorbell. From inside she heard faint music. She caught a glimpse of her reflection in the window—a pretty girl all in red with a present under her arm.

Something wonderful is going to happen to me, she thought. She pressed the bell again, and the twins' mother came to the door, slim and elegant. "Hello, Lena. Let me take your present."

Lena handed her the gift. From the other room the voices of boys and girls rose over loud party music.

"Go right in," said the twins' mother. "Everyone's here already."

Lena smoothed the skirt of her dress, touched her hair, took a quick peek into the dark massive mirror on the wall, and entered the party.

The living room was decorated with blue and red balloons and crepe streamers. The girls had settled themselves decorously on the gray couch by the window and were talking and laughing a little louder than usual.

They were wearing starched dresses with crinoline petticoats underneath and had curled their hair so that it flipped either up or down. Everyone was wearing nylon stockings and shiny black patent leather shoes with little heels.

Lena had worn white ankle socks and flat Mary Janes.

On the other couch the boys—Arthur, Jonathan, Peter, Stewart, Paul, and Wayne— had short hair slicked back from clean faces. In white shirts and creased pants, they elbowed one another and whispered. All except Stewart, who sat straight and pale and serious, not talking, not looking at anyone.

Arthur said something in a low voice, and the other boys laughed loudly and stared at the girls.

Lena flushed, as though the laughter were meant for her.

"Hi, Lena!" Catherine Mary and Mary Catherine came up on either side of her. They wore identical blue velvet dresses with cream-colored trim and matching blue slippers. "What did you get us?"

"You'll see."

"We've already gotten headbands in three colors and matching blouses," said the twins. "And some real cologne and bath powder."

"I got lilac," said Catherine Mary.

"Violet for me," said Mary Catherine.

"You better have gotten us something good," they chorused.

"You'll like the color," said Lena. She was starting to feel uneasy. Did the twins even like to read?

"Is it soap?" asked Mary Catherine.

"Lipstick?" asked her sister.

"A sweater?"

Lena shook her head. The birthday present she had so carefully picked out was all wrong. The twins didn't want fairy tales. They wanted makeup and nylons and necklaces with purple stones and high-heeled slippers. They wanted hair curlers and angora sweaters, rings from boys and phone calls at night.

Soon they would be in sixth grade. And there would be dances and more parties. There would be pledges and gifts and dates at skating rinks.

Stewart Pine was staring at her from the opposite side of the room.

"Lena," he said.

She thought of the last time they had been together. It was at the supermarket after he had been caught. The clerk had let him go, and they had walked home silently together. As they approached her house he had looked at her and spoken one word: "Sorry."

Lena hadn't known what to say. She had ducked her head and run up the stairs to her porch. She and Stewart hadn't seen each other much since then.

Now she wished they were together again, walking along Moose Street.

She leaned forward. "Stewart . . ."

"Game time, boys and girls." The twins' grandmother, in her long black dress with a lace shawl, came slowly into the room holding a silver tray. "Now, everyone take a piece of paper and a pencil. The twins will hand them out."

"Yes, Grandmother," said Mary Catherine and Catherine Mary.

"We are going to play scrambled-word games," said their grandmother. "Won't that be fun for you and your little friends?"

"Yes, Grandmother," said Mary Catherine and Catherine Mary.

The grandmother sat on one of the heavy mahogany chairs and watched the twins hand out pencils and paper. "Whoever gets the most words out of these letters," she said, "will win a prize."

"I'll win it," announced Danette. She had crossed her legs in their new nylon stockings at the ankles, the way the home economics teacher had taught them last week.

"Nicely bred young ladies never cross their legs at the knees," the teacher had told them. "And their skirts always cover their knees."

Danette looked very ladylike.

Lena looked down at her paper. Danette was not going to win. This was something Lena knew how to do and do well.

"How many words can you make out of these seven letters, boys and girls?" asked the grandmother, smoothing the dull black material of her dress.

The letters EPMLAOH were written at the top of the page. Lena began to write. *Map, lap, hop, mop, meal, peal, heal, heap, lam, ham, home, loam, poem, mope, lope, male, pale, hale, lame, hem . . .*

Lena glanced at Danette, who had filled her page with words and was writing as fast as she could.

"No cheating!" said Danette, shielding her page with her arm.

"I'm not cheating!" Lena protested. She bent back over her paper. *Elm, alm, oh, ah, helm,* she wrote.

"I have twenty-five words," Danette announced.

"Wow. Twenty-five," said Pauline, who was sitting next to Danette. "I only have ten."

"Twenty-nine!" said Arthur. "I've got twenty-nine."

"You're *so* smart," Danette told him. She took a lipstick out of her pocket and ran it lightly over her lips.

Help, pole, mole, hole, lop, palm, wrote Lena. "Thirty-one!" she called triumphantly.

"The winner!" shouted Catherine Mary. "The brain of our class, Lena Rosen!"

Nancy applauded. Pauline, who was thin and sharp like a needle, stared.

And Danette said, "She must have cheated. Arthur should have won."

"I did *not* cheat!" said Lena.

"Don't worry," said Danette. "We know you didn't cheat, Lena. You have twice as many brains as you need anyway. That's why your head is so big."

The twins and the other girls laughed loudly, while the boys snickered.

For the second time that day, Lena felt her face go hot.

"And here is the prize," said Mary Catherine, putting a small black book into Lena's hand. "We hope you like it and will use it."

Lena looked down at the book. Stamped in gold letters were the words *A Child's Book of Prayers*. On the inside page was a picture of Jesus with a curly brown beard and sorrowful eyes.

The twins smiled sweetly, while their grandmother nodded approval from the mahogany chair.

"Thanks," Lena mumbled, and shoved the book into her pocket.

"Time for cake and presents!" The twins' slender and pretty mother came into the living room bearing a large iced cake with blue and pink flowers and striped candles burning brightly. "Happy birthday to you!" she sang.

The others joined in. Lena sang, her face still burning. Do I really have a big head? she wondered. She tried to catch a glimpse of herself in the mirror on the other side of the room, but it was mounted too high.

"Happy birthday, dear twins," she sang with the others, gawky and awkward in the white ankle socks that kept falling down, her straight hair that would not flip up properly, and the messy sash that had already come untied . . . "Happy birthday to you."

"Make a wish, twins," said their mother.

The twins clasped hands and shut their eyes tight.

And Lena wished . . . She wished herself in a world of fountains and light and roses, where joy and delight flowed like water, where beauty and grace were hers.

Perhaps she had only to open a door, and there it would be. I will find that world someday, she promised herself.

The twins whispered together and smiled at their friends, then leaned over the cake and blew out the candles. "We wish that every day would be as much fun as this one."

Everyone clapped.

The grandmother smiled.

The twins' mother picked up the knife and began to slice the cake.

Red Rover, Red Rover

The sun was warm for an early October day. Lena flew along the sidewalk, her new navy coat billowing with the wind, her cheeks red, black hair sweeping around her face. She was smiling to herself, jumping over cracks, kicking her feet into brightly colored piles of leaves and watching them float through the air. "Step on a crack, break your mother's back," she sang as though she were still in second grade instead of in sixth.

Ahead of her, Esther Brown trudged down

Moose Street, her arms full of books, shapeless socks falling around her ankles.

At the schoolyard gate Esther paused for a moment. Then she walked slowly forward.

Lena followed Esther into the schoolyard.

They were waiting for Esther: Danette, with her round face and staring black eyes; the twins, Mary Catherine and Catherine Mary, in matching dresses of red and white; Pauline, who was small and thin and fierce; and a few others. They stood in two lines hitting their books like drums, chanting at first softly, and then louder and louder as she approached:

> "Esther Brown, Esther Brown,
> Greasy hair,
> You look like a clown!"

Esther came to an uncertain halt in front of the girls.

Lena watched as Danette grabbed Esther

and shoved her down the middle of the aisle formed by the chanting girls.

"Esther Brown, Esther Brown,
    You're a clown;
    Fall down!" sang the girls.

"Phew!" said Pauline, holding her small freckled nose. "She stinks."

"Do you ever take a bath, Esther?" asked Mary Catherine.

"When her mother needs some cooking oil, she wrings out Esther's hair," said Danette.

Esther kept her head down as though she didn't hear them.

"Please, let me through," Esther muttered.

"What do you think?" Danette asked the other girls, her round moon face triumphant. Her black eyes scanned the playground and came to rest on Lena. "Shall we let her through?"

Lena fumbled with her books, pretending she hadn't heard, hadn't seen.

"Make her take a bath first," suggested Catherine Mary.

Danette eyed a nearby mud puddle.

"No!" Esther said.

A loud clanging came from the school. "Saved by the bell," said Danette. She gave Esther one final shove, then linked arms with the twins and headed inside.

Lena followed the girls, walking quickly past Esther.

The second bell was ringing, and the children had already settled themselves as Esther arrived in class, two bright red spots burning on her cheeks.

"Almost late again, Esther," said Mrs. Wesley, the sixth-grade teacher. She was tall and angular and reminded Lena of a rake. "Get your coat off now."

Lena watched as Esther disappeared into the cloakroom, then came out again.

Her shoulders hunched, she sat at her desk and pulled out paper, a pencil, and an eraser.

"*Ssssst*, Esther!" It was Danette, tapping on her desk.

Esther turned. "What do you want?"

While Esther's back was turned, Mary Catherine darted over and grabbed the pencil from her desk.

Danette stared hard at Esther. "Your dress is unzipped."

Esther clutched her dress. "It isn't," she said.

"It's time for the spelling test," said Mrs. Wesley. "Hands on the desk. Paper and pencil ready."

Esther looked wildly around the room.

"Where's your pencil, Esther?" asked Mrs. Wesley.

Everyone sat very straight and serious at their desks.

"Someone must have taken it," Esther said.

"Here, have mine," said Mary Catherine

in a concerned voice. Esther took one look at the pencil and snatched it out of Mary Catherine's hand.

Danette smirked. Esther raised her eyes and met Lena's gaze. Lena turned her head away.

In gym that day, Mrs. Wesley's class joined the other sixth-grade class in the schoolyard.

For a few minutes everyone ran free, kicking stones and chasing one another up to the wire fence.

"Time for games!" called the teacher.

They made two long lines that faced each other. Clutching wrists, they formed two human chains that stretched across the gravel of the schoolyard.

Danette was captain of one team, which had Mary Catherine, Lena, and Pauline on it.

A boy named John from the other class was captain of the opposing team, which had Stewart Pine, Nancy, Esther, and Catherine Mary.

"Red rover, red rover, let Nancy come over," called Danette.

Nancy ran hard and crashed into Danette and Mary Catherine, but she didn't break their grip. She joined their team.

"Red rover, red rover, let Pauline come over," called John.

Pauline headed straight for Esther, who was holding the wrist of a fat boy with red hair. As Pauline smashed into Esther's outstretched arm Esther let go, and Pauline broke through.

"Hooray, Pauline!" shouted Lena's team.

They had found the weak link. One after another they ran at Esther. They flung themselves on her, even when she dropped her arm before they hit her.

Her face twisted. She grimaced and pulled away. When the gym teacher passed, Esther raised her hand. "Can I be excused?"

"No excuses," he said. "Hold the line."

Danette's black eyes sparkled and her red lips curved in a smile.

It was Lena's turn. "Red rover, red rover, let Lena come over!"

"Go, Lena!" yelled her team. "Kill!"

Lena stumbled forward, turning automatically toward Esther and the boy next to her, who looked embarrassed and annoyed.

"Get her, Lena!" screamed Danette.

"Do it!" shouted Pauline.

As she ran, Lena glanced at Esther's pale, sweating face, and suddenly she hated her. She hated Esther's stringy hair and her ugly dresses. She hated Esther's fear and her misery and her weakness.

And she wanted to hurt her, break her bones, pull her hair, kick her pale flabby limbs. And more: Lena wanted to crush her completely, annihilate that pleading, miserable face.

Lena lifted her eyes and met Esther's terrified stare straight on.

And she saw herself as Esther must see her—fists clenched, jaw tight, eyes glaring. As Esther, she saw sharp gravel and hard blue sky.

She saw a line of jeering, taunting faces.

The few feet of gravel between her team and the other seemed to shrink and expand at the same time. The distance she had to run was both too near and too far.

At the last minute Lena turned aside and crashed into the fat boy, who held steady.

"Boo!" yelled her team. "Boo, Lena!"

"Why didn't you hit her?" someone yelled. "What are you afraid of?"

Lena turned aside, exhausted. She didn't look at Esther. She didn't look at Nancy. She didn't look at Danette.

She didn't cheer when her team won.

The Secret House

One day Lena came back from lunch to find a stack of small white envelopes inside her school desk. She slid the envelopes onto her lap so Mrs. Wesley would not see them and opened them one by one.

Although it was November, Stewart had sent her valentines.

I LOVE YOU, said the first one. BE MINE, said the second and the third and the fourth. The fifth, sixth, seventh, and eighth said: I ♡ YOU. And on the remaining four cards he had simply written in block letters, MY VALENTINE.

They were signed: STEWART, SP, or YOURS FOREVER, STEWART PINE.

Lena looked up. Stewart sat at the front of the class. He had twisted around in his seat and was watching her. Mrs. Wesley walked by. "Face front!" she said.

That afternoon Stewart was waiting for Lena after school. He stood by the school gate on Moose Street, and when she came out, he followed her silently home. She laughed and talked with Nancy more loudly than usual. She let her newly cut hair swing around her face. She even took Nancy's arm and skipped past Catalano's candy store.

In class next day Stewart kept craning his head to look at her—which earned him slaps from Mrs. Wesley. He would turn his head and smile at Lena or wink at her as though this were a special show that he was putting on for her benefit.

At the end of the day Lena came out of the

schoolyard alone. Stewart was waiting. "Come home with me," he said.

"Is your stepfather going to be there?" Lena asked.

"No, he's never there."

Lena thought of Stewart stumbling down the steps last fall, his cheek bright red.

"No one will be there," said Stewart. "I promise."

The wind was whipping around her legs. It was cold. Already her toes were numb. She thought of hot chocolate waiting at home. But she also thought of twelve red valentines sitting in her coat pocket. "Okay," she said.

They walked down Moose Street, turned a corner, and then another. And then they were back at the school.

"I thought we were going to your house," said Lena. "This is the wrong direction."

"You'll see," said Stewart.

He led her into the schoolyard and through a door at the back of the school.

"Why are we here?" Lena asked. "Where are you taking me?"

"Come on. We don't want to get caught." Stewart started running up the hard marble stairs.

Lena's toes were still numb from the cold, and her boots left a trail of slush. Up stairs, down corridors, past mysterious closed doors, and finally, on the third and topmost floor of the school, Stewart opened the door to the special projects room.

He held his finger to his lips. From somewhere in the building Lena heard the scratchy sounds of the janitor's radio being played.

In the special projects room there were black sewing machines on tables and dressmakers' models draped with lengths of cloth.

"We're not supposed to be here," Lena whispered.

Stewart led the way. They tiptoed past shadowy desks and darkened bulletin boards. In the back of the room Stewart took a key off a hook and unlocked a small red door. . . .

And Lena saw, for the first time, the house within the school.

There was the living room, with a gray couch and matching chairs. There were bookcases, a newspaper on a table, and a pair of slippers in front of a stuffed red plush chair.

Lena peered into the kitchen. "Oh!" she whispered. It had a stove and refrigerator, a table and chairs, and the prettiest blue curtains with lace ruffles on them.

The bedroom had a real bed with yellow sheets and a matching bedspread. Lena went over to the drawers and carefully opened one. It was filled with towels, clean and folded.

It was the most perfect cozy little home.

Stewart stood by the window. "There he goes," he said. "We're safe now."

Lena looked out the window with the lace curtains and saw in the schoolyard below the tall thin figure of the janitor in his black overcoat heading toward Moose Street.

Then she turned back to the kitchen and began opening drawers, examining silverware, peering into cupboards. Stewart took off his boots, hung his coat in the closet, then leaned back on the couch and watched her, a proud smile on his face.

He got up and went to the refrigerator. "I thought so. Home ec this afternoon." He set a platter of fried chicken legs on the table. He rummaged in the drawers, pulled out plates and forks and knives, and set the table. "Let's eat."

"Do you come here a lot?" Lena asked him.

"I do this all the time. Once I slept here." His eyes were shining, his thin white face touched with color.

Lena sat down at the table.

"Have a chicken leg," said Stewart.

"Thank you, I will."

"Delicious," he said. "You are a wonderful cook."

"Thank you," said Lena. "It's my special recipe."

"What's for dessert?"

"Let me see." Lena got up and opened the refrigerator. There was half a chocolate cake with pink rosettes on it. "I made something you like. Devil's food cake!"

"My favorite," said Stewart.

She sliced them both large pieces.

They washed and dried the dishes together. Lena put on a red polka-dotted apron she found on a hook. Stewart dried with a white linen cloth. They put the dishes away. They put back the fried chicken ("No one will know," said Stewart) and the cake ("They'll think one of the teachers snuck in and ate it"), and they wiped the floor where their boots had tracked in slush.

"What a wonderful house," said Lena. "I'm glad you brought me here."

"And it's ours," Stewart told her. "We can come whenever we want."

When they got to the bottom of the stairs, the doors of the school were chained shut.

Lena's heart began to beat faster. What if they were locked in the school for the night? What would her parents say? What would the teachers and principal do when they found the two of them the next morning?

"Come on," said Stewart. He led her into another room and pushed open a window.

Lena climbed onto the window sill and slowly let herself down onto the sidewalk.

No one was in sight.

Then Stewart climbed out, shut the window, and jumped down beside her.

"Tomorrow we'll come again," he said.

"Tomorrow?" she said. As they walked across the gravel schoolyard Lena saw clearly the danger ahead. She saw herself caught, hauled to the principal's office, displayed as a troublemaker in front of everyone.

At the gate, they paused. "Tomorrow?" he asked.

Stewart took the blows and scoldings of the teachers and shrugged them off, but she would not be able to bear it.

Lena shook her head.

"The day after, then."

Lena hesitated. The house hidden in the school and its joys and pleasures seemed to dissolve like a dream or a memory from long ago.

"I'll come when I can," she said at last.

"Come soon," said Stewart.

"Yes," said Lena. "I will." But she knew she would never go back to the secret house.

Christmas Story

The Rosens were celebrating the eight days of Hanukkah, but all around them was Christmas.

The church across from the school was garlanded with spruce and velvet bows and golden bells, and the school was decorated with long strips of candy canes, painted wooden Christmas trees, and tissue-paper angels dotted with little gold sprinkles.

PEACE ON EARTH, GOODWILL TO ALL read the banners hanging from the school windows.

The houses of Moose Street were wreathed

in spruce and strung from roof to basement with brightly colored lights. Tall trees laden with ornaments glowed from behind curtained windows. Giant red bows were tied on doors and mailboxes and lampposts. Life-size cardboard Santas driving sleighs full of presents waved from porches.

In the attic apartment where Nancy and her mother lived the living room was hung with silver tinsel and gold stars. A little white angel perched on top of a thick green tree; the room was warm and smelled of spice and orange and evergreen. One night Nancy and Lena strung tiny red cranberries and fat white popcorn on thread to hang on the tree in long graceful loops.

The richness of Christmas!

By contrast, Hanukkah seemed plain and unadorned. To be sure, it lasted eight days. Lena told Nancy, "We get a present every day!" Her family started with small presents, like crayons and paper, and worked their way up through games, dolls, and finally on the last night, the biggest one of all—a painting set, a sled, or even a bicycle.

"That sounds like fun," Nancy replied. Then she added, "We get more than eight presents on just one day!"

"Isn't that too much all at once?" Lena asked, hoping that Nancy would tell her that yes, at the end of the day she had a headache, a stomachache, and was thoroughly sick of toys and family.

"It's great!"

"One a day is enough for me," Lena said firmly. But she thought with longing of Christmas trees heaped with presents, of stockings overflowing with oranges and chocolates and wooden puppets and jacks, of tables laden with roasts and cakes and pies and spiced cider.

On the third day of Hanukkah, Lena walked into the classroom and saw a crowd of chil-

dren around the bulletin board. Mrs. Wesley
had tacked up a photograph of a family gathered around a lighted menorah. MR. AND MRS.
SHULMAN CELEBRATE HANUKKAH, said the cap-
tion.

Mr. Shulman wore a skullcap and had re-
ceding hair and a double chin. He was light-
ing the candles with a special candle called a
shammes. Mrs. Shulman stood proudly at his
side, plump and motherly with round black
eyes.

The three Shulman children, devout and
serious, watched their parents. The boys, in
suits and skullcaps, had pale pointed faces.
Their sister, plump like her mother, wore her
hair tightly braided around her head and
smiled adoringly at her brothers.

"Just like your family," said Nancy sar-
castically.

"Yeah, right." Lena thought of her tall thin
father, who never wore a skullcap and had

bright red hair. Her mother, who was slim and wore nice clothes. Her blue-eyed sister. And herself—she had dark hair and blue eyes, but she was thin and had red cheeks.

"Lena, is that how your family celebrates Hanukkah?" Danette asked brightly.

"Do you go to church on Hanukkah?" asked Arthur, who was holding Danette's hand secretly so that Mrs. Wesley wouldn't see.

"It's called a synagogue," said Lena. "And we don't go."

"If you don't go to church, how do you know you're Jewish?" asked Danette.

"I was born into it," said Lena.

Mrs. Wesley rang a bell, and all the boys and girls filed to their desks. "I hope everyone found our bulletin board very educational." She clapped her hands twice. "Time for music rehearsal," she announced.

"Hey, Lena," said Nancy in the hall later.

"Can I come to Hanukkah at your house to-night?"

Lena stared at her. "Why?"

"It would be fun. Don't you think so?"

Lena imagined Nancy in her house watching her father say the blessings awkwardly and quickly. Seeing Lena rip open her solitary present. And then would they play with the wooden dreidels that seemed so babyish now that Lena was in sixth grade? Or share a handful of chocolate coins that they'd unwrap and eat in a few moments?

"I'll have to ask my mother," Lena said.

"She'll let me! I know she will! Your mother will say yes."

Lena knew it was true. Her mother would invite Nancy over, would probably say, "Why didn't we think of this before?"

They tramped into the other sixth-grade classroom and sat in chairs placed along the rows of desks. Lena was next to a girl with dark brown ringlets and a freckled face whose name was Marlene.

The two teachers stood at the front of the classroom and raised their hands. "Now, boys and girls," they said.

The class sang. They sang "Silent Night," "It Came Upon a Midnight Clear," "Santa Claus Is Coming to Town," and "Hark! The Herald Angels Sing." They sang "Frosty the Snowman," "Jingle Bells," "O Tannenbaum," and "O Little Town of Bethlehem."

Lena and her family had passed through Bethlehem, Pennsylvania, one snowy night. And from then on, whenever she heard about the town of Bethlehem, Lena didn't see the stable in the Holy Land, but thought of dark, slippery roads and snow drifting to the ground by the drugstore window where they had stopped to buy cups of hot chocolate.

When the class sang "Joy to the world, the Lord is come," Lena mouthed the words.

"He is not *my* lord," she said to herself. To her, he was just a little baby with a gold plate on his head.

"How come you're not singing?" whispered Marlene.

Lena looked at her for a moment. "I'm Jewish."

"Oh. I thought you lived on Moose Street."

"I do."

Marlene took up the song again, but from time to time darted curious glances at Lena.

Lena thought of her house on Moose Street—the large rooms stacked one on top of another, the scarred wooden floors, the big windows through which she watched the snow, the cars, the neighbors.

In the dining room that night her family would gather around the table.

First came the blessing.

Then her mother would light the menorah. It was a blue and silver menorah from

Israel that her grandmother had sent them. They would light the candles that Lena picked out of the box—blue and yellow and red and white, while her father recited another blessing.

Then her uncle would give her some Hanukkah gelt—either chocolate coins or money for her bank.

And Lena would open her present—maybe the Monopoly game she had asked for?—and her mother and father and uncle would sit around the table talking and laughing and drinking small glasses of golden wine.

My family, Lena thought.

She would put ribbons in Deedee's hair, and Deedee would twirl around and around, until she fell down.

From across the room Nancy gave a little wave and with her lips formed the word *tonight*.

And Lena nodded.

She would let her happiness grow inside her all day.

By night it would be strong, and she would open the door to her house and invite her friend in.

Moose Street Sleeps

Moose Street sleeps. A light wind rustles the leaves of the maple and chestnut trees. The air smells faintly of gasoline. And the bells of St. Mary's ring out every fifteen minutes. "Sleep, sleep, sleep . . ." they say.

Lena is sleeping in her white bed next to the window. The breeze sways the venetian blinds and ruffles Lena's hair as she dreams of floating over the city in a long pink nightgown.

Deedee sleeps in her crib in the glass porch, her chubby fist curled around her green toothbrush. Lena's mother and father sleep in their room at the other end of the house.

Lena's former teacher, Miss Fulman, who lives alone on the other side of Moose Street, sits on her porch and knits a scarf for next winter. Her knitting needles click while she rocks back and forth, back and forth on the wooden porch.

The two ancient ladies next door, the Gilly sisters, are sleeping in their violet-scented rooms—or are they? A light shines all night long from behind gauzy curtains in their dining room.

Lena's best friend Nancy sleeps in the attic apartment she shares with her mother two blocks away on Moose Street.

Lena's worst enemy Danette sleeps in her red room with its canopy bed and large blue dollhouse with real wooden furniture.

Esther Brown sleeps too. Who knows where? She has no friends and has never invited anyone to her home.

Stewart Pine sleeps in the bed he shares with his older brother Sam in the house behind the motorcycle shop. His brother kicks him in his sleep, and Stewart mutters, but he doesn't awaken.

The twins, Catherine Mary and Mary Catherine, are asleep in their prim twin beds of pink and white.

The school on Moose Street—the massive brick building with two entrances, one for boys and the other for girls—sleeps too. The worn floors gleam in the darkness. The gashed desks with their piles of books and papers cast long shadows along the walls of the class-rooms. The big ugly school is silent.

An occasional car still passes on the street, and if Lena were awake she would watch its headlights glide over the wall, then across the ceiling of her room. The light illuminates the shelf of books above her head and some clay figures on her desk. Then it disappears. The room is dark again.

The wind blows through the silky leaves of the maple trees. It passes over the vacant lot at the end of Moose Street—the vacant lot that was once a cemetery, where Lena sometimes finds half-buried gravestones in the grass. The wind passes over the row of crooked houses on Moose Street, their porches filled with carriages, bikes, washtubs, Hula-Hoops. . . . And it rustles the leaves of the trees in Lena's yard.

The wind blows through Lena's window, over her sleeping face, bringing with it a faint scent of gasoline and flowers. The bells of St. Mary's ring out the hour.

And Moose Street sleeps. . . .

ANNE MAZER grew up in a family of writers in Syracuse, N.Y., the setting for *Moose Street*. Intending to be an artist, she studied at the School of Visual and Performing Arts at Syracuse University. She then went to the Sorbonne, in Paris, where she studied French literature, and where she started writing. She is the author of *Watch Me,* illustrated by Stacey Schuett, *The Yellow Button,* illustrated by Judy Pedersen, and *The Salamander Room,* illustrated by Steve Johnson.

She lives with her husband and two children in northeastern Pennsylvania.